ADVENTURES

RESCUE IN KENYA

By Judith Marie Austin
Illustrations by Virgina Kylberg
and a compendium of other GlobalFriends artists

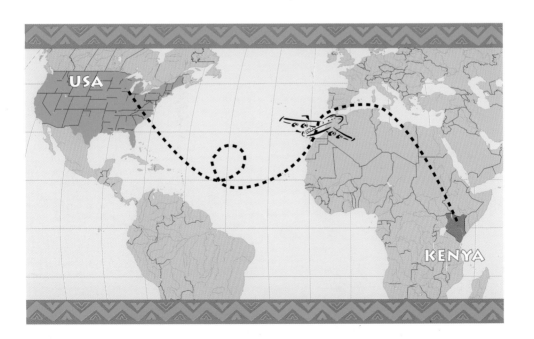

Everyone Smiles in the Same Language

Published by GlobalFriends Press

© *1997 GlobalFriends Collection, Inc.*

First Edition
Printed in Korea

For more information contact:
Book Editor, GlobalFriends Press
1820 Gateway Drive, Suite 320
San Mateo, CA 94404

ISBN: #1-58056-006-7

Welcome to Kenya

"Awesome!" Marissa was staring out the bus window with her nose pressed against the glass as they drove past a gigantic waterfall.

Briana turned around to look. "That must be Thomson's Falls. Akua wrote to me about it."

"When are we gonna get there? To Nakuru, I mean. I want to meet Akua!" Marissa exclaimed.

Briana glanced at the guidebook, scanning the page. She loved reading and discovering new things. "It can't be much further," she realized. "We're already in the Rift Valley. "

"I didn't think Kenya would be like this." Marissa wiped her nose print off the window.

Briana looked up. "What did you expect?"

"Jungle, I guess." Marissa shrugged. "Like a Tarzan movie."

"Most of Kenya is grassland, it's called a savannah. That's why they have so many animals. They graze on the grass." Briana grinned.

"I think all the animals are totally cool!" Marissa exclaimed. "Wow! Look at those zebras!"

A herd of zebras was racing along the top of a ridge, kicking up clouds of dust and rocks.

"We're coming into Nakuru now," Briana's mom, announced from the bus seat in back of them.

"Briana, do you know what Akua looks like?" Marissa asked.

"I've got a photograph somewhere." Briana was digging through her backpack. "Here it is!"

Marissa looked at the worn photo. A pretty Kenyan girl was smiling and wearing a colorful headwrap. She had long dark hair and beautiful brown eyes.

"Now I know who to look for. The prettiest girl in the crowd."

Excited, Marissa nudged Briana. "Do you think there'll be a crowd at the bus depot?"

Briana nodded thoughtfully. "Probably."

There was! A group of people crowded up as their bus pulled in. Briana picked out Akua right away. "There she is!"

"Jambo!" Akua shouted as they stepped off the bus. She threw her arms around Briana. "You must be Briana!"

Briana hugged her back. "I'm so glad to finally meet you!" She grabbed Marissa. "This is Marissa," she introduced eagerly, "and my mom, and this is Marissa's mom! We're all so glad to finally be here!"

"This is awesome!" Marissa joined the hug, dancing on her

tiptoes. "I love your country!"

Smiling, Akua's mother stepped up. "Jambo and welcome. Akua and I have waited so long to finally meet you. Could I help to carry anything? Our *matatu* is waiting." She gestured to the brightly painted minibus.

They made a short stop at the Waterbuck Hotel in Nakuru to drop off their luggage, then traveled on to Lake Nakuru.

On the shore, Marissa pointed across the lake. "What's all that pink stuff?" She grabbed Briana. "Look! It's moving!"

"Flamingos," Akua explained. "Sometimes there are as many as two million." Akua was a real nature-lover. She knew all her country's animals and birds on sight.

"Two million flamingos! Awesome!" Marissa was dancing on her tiptoes again.

"They say that Lake Nakuru is the most spectacular bird sanctuary in the world." Usually quiet and shy, Akua couldn't help being proud of her country. The wind blew across the lake, bringing the sound of several hundred thousand flamingos grunting and honking.

Briana turned around. "What's that?"

Akua grinned. "The flamingos. They are very noisy."

"Can we walk over there?" Briana asked, eager to explore.

Akua shook her head. "No. You can only get out of a vehicle here and at certain viewpoints around the lake."

Marissa looked puzzled. "How come?"

"We're inside the Lake Nakuru National Park boundaries, and the law is for your protection. There is no hunting anywhere in Kenya, but we have many wild animals. If you're inside a vehicle, they can't hurt you." Akua was smiling.

"We could take the van around the lake, right?" Briana asked anxiously. She wanted to see everything.

"You mean the *matatu?* Yes, of course," Akua assured.

"That's good! I don't want to miss anything!" Briana was staring up in the sky.

Marissa looked up. "What do you see?"

Briana pointed. "Those guys. They're not pink so they can't be flamingos."

Akua followed their gaze. "Those birds are vultures."

"Vultures!" Briana gasped.

Akua circled an arm around her. She knew just how to comfort Briana. "Vultures won't hurt you," she said soothingly.

Assured, Briana was still gazing. "They don't fly very well."

Akua shook her head, sharing her knowledge of nature. "Vultures are very poor flyers. They can't fly at all after eating."

"I didn't know that," Marissa commented.

A group of *Masai* women walked past. They were dressed in flowing kanga wraps and beautiful collar necklaces.

Akua explained "Those are *Masai*. The *Masai* are an ethnic group who farm for a living. They are wonderful people."

Marissa was enchanted. "I love their dresses and their jewelry."

"The *Masai* wear brightly colored pieces of cloth, called *rubeka*. And each of their colorful necklaces is made from hundreds of beads. Aren't they beautiful?" Akua had many friends who were *Masai* who worked with her at the animal orphanage.

They were speaking a different language. Briana and Marissa listened intently.

"What language is that?" Marissa whispered.

"It is what you call Swahili..." Akua started.

"What do *you* call it?"

"*Kiswahili*. It's our official language. English is our second language. Almost everyone speaks English."

"No wonder you sound so American. It's kinda weird though, the way you sound so American when Kenya doesn't look like America at all." Marissa was gazing across the lake at the huge flock of flamingos again.

"It sure doesn't look like Chicago." Briana couldn't imagine a skyscraper in Kenya. "Well, Nairobi maybe."

Akua was thinking. "Nairobi is a very big city."

"Yeah, when we landed at the airport, Nairobi did kinda look like Chicago," Briana mused.

Akua nodded. "Nairobi is smaller perhaps, but it is a wonderful city for the latest in movies, bookshops, hotels and restaurants. Much business is done there. There are huge buildings, and the traffic is very bad."

Briana laughed. "Now that does sound like Chicago!"

Akua's mother laughed. "Don't worry. Kenya doesn't have many big cities. Nakuru is our fourth largest city, and it is very, very small compared to big cities in America."

"Good!" Marissa exclaimed. "I didn't come to see cities."

"I came to see exactly what we're seeing. Animals and birds and tribal people." Briana was grinning too. "Hey, mom? Tell me again what tribe our ancestors were from!"

Beth smoothed Briana's hair. "The *El-Molo* tribe from around Lake Turkana."

"Oh, yeah. *El-Molo,*" Briana murmured.

"You never told me you were from a real tribe in Africa!" Marissa exclaimed. "That's so cool!"

"All Black Americans have descended from a tribe somewhere," Briana explained. "That's really why we had to come to Kenya. I love my heritage and ancestry."

"Welcome home to Kenya," Akua said simply.

A Picnic on Lake Nakuru

"What's that?" Briana asked, eager to try it.

"It is a fried yam. What you call a sweet potato." Akua put one on Briana's plate.

"These wood dishes are awesome!" Marissa was holding onto a spoon carved into a giraffe. She'd already decided she liked Kenyan tea. It was about half milk and super sweet.

The girls and their mothers were enjoying a picnic on Lake Nakuru. From where they sprawled, they could hear the flamingos honking and carrying on.

"Does everybody in Africa celebrate Kwanzaa next week?" Marissa set down her corn cob.

Akua looked puzzled. "What's Kwanzaa?"

"Kwanzaa is an African <u>American</u> holiday," Briana explained.

"Oh!" Marissa was confused. "I thought it was African."

"No," Briana was thinking of the best way to explain Kwanzaa. "It celebrates our African heritage."

Akua was surprised. "That's interesting! Can you tell me about it?"

Briana started eagerly. "It's a celebration for African Americans to have pride in their African heritage. Kwanzaa lasts for a whole week between Christmas and New Year's."

"And there are symbols like the Kinara," she went on. "That's a candle-holder that holds seven candles. The seven candles represent the seven principles of Kwanzaa."

"Seven principles? What are they?" Akua was intrigued.

Briana thought for a moment. "Unity is the first principle. Self determination, being yourself and thinking for yourself is the second one. The third one is working together to help other people, and the fourth one is sharing the wealth. The fifth principle is having a purpose in what you do. Being creative is the sixth one, and having faith is the last one. Living every day by the seven principles allows you to get the most out of life."

"That sounds wonderful. I believe in all those principles," Akua contributed softly, "especially working together. That's why I volunteer with my *Masai* friends at the Nairobi Animal Orphanage. like to work with other people to help the baby animals."

"An animal orphanage!"

"Can we help too?" Briana pleaded.

Akua smiled. "Of course." She knew the Animal Orphanage needed many workers every day.

"Cool! What do you do?" Marissa was even more excited.

"Sometimes I feed the baby animals, and sometimes I clean their pens. I fill the water bowls. Sometimes I help to capture orphaned babies," Akua explained.

"What kind of baby animals?" Marissa pressed.

"All kinds. Zebras, antelopes, gazelles, impala, giraffes and water buffalo. Cats like cheetahs, civets and genets. A few hyenas and jackals. Last week the *Masai* brought in a baby lion that they found abandoned and hurt. Usually the *Masai* do not go near lions because the lions attack their cattle. But this one was in trouble and the Masai care very much about the wildlife."

Akua continued, "Sometimes we take in a leopard or lion. We

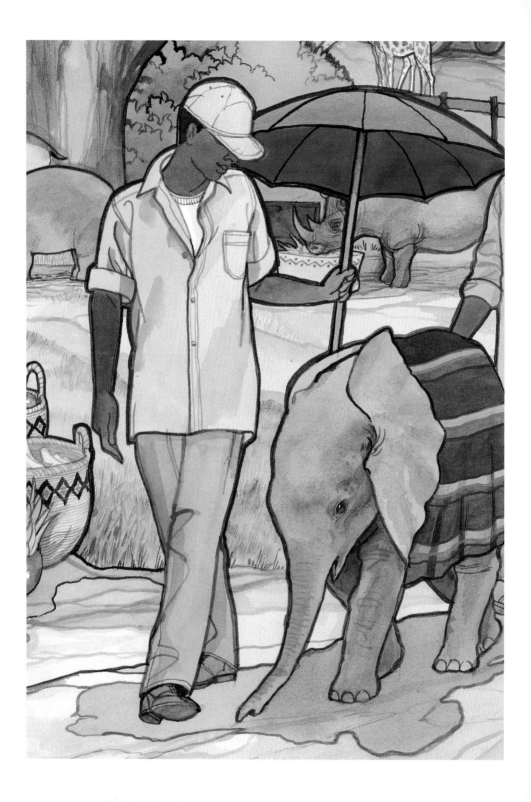

don't get many rhinoceros because they're good at coming up with substitute mothers. So are wart hogs and any of the monkeys like colobus and bushbabies."

"What's your favorite animal?" Briana wanted to know.

Akua loved all animals so it was a hard question to answer. "A *twiga*, I think. Oh, a *twiga* is a giraffe. They are very large, but very gentle."

"I've got a really cool idea!" Marissa couldn't stop thinking about Kwanzaa. "Let's practice the Kwanzaa principle of Unity by helping each other at the Animal Orphanage. This is gonna be totally awesome!"

Feeding the Baby Animals

The three friends were inside a feeding station at the Nairobi Animal Orphanage. "What do you feed baby zebras?" Briana was eager to know.

Akua pulled down a large bottle of white powder from one of the shelves. "This. It's a milk substitute, my *rafiki*." She held out the bottle. "You mix it half water and half powder. Fill these bottles. We'll need ten."

"*Rafiki?*" Briana questioned, taking the bottle.

Akua smiled shyly. "*Rafiki* is *Kiswahili* for friend."

"Am I folding these right?" Marissa called from the far corner of the hut. She was folding animal blankets.

Akua glanced over. "Yes, that's exactly right. Over once, then over again. Just stack them by the entrance."

"Do the babies need blankets to keep warm?" Briana asked from where she was stirring the powdered milk formula.

Akua smiled. "Sometimes, if it gets cold at night. They have no

mother to keep them warm, you see. Sometimes we use them for babies who need protection from the sun, like the baby *kifarus*, rhinos, who have no fur to protect their skin."

The stack of unfolded blankets seemed to be growing. Marissa's arms were getting tired. Akua could see that she was slowing down. "Would you help Briana fill the bottles? I could finish the blankets," she offered.

Marissa brightened. "Sure!"

With the three girls working as a team, the baby bottles and blankets were done in no time.

"Now for the fun part," Akua announced. "Take three bottles apiece. That's right. I'll take four. Now walk this way."

Akua led the way out of the feeding station hut toward the baby zebra pen. "When you're feeding the *punda milia*, I mean zebras, keep the bottle tipped above their head so they have to reach up for it. Like they would for their mother's milk. And be careful!" She giggled. "Sometimes they can be very greedy. Don't let them pull the bottle from your hand. Here, put the extra bottles on this bench, so you're only taking in one with you. Otherwise the *punda milia* will try to steal them from you!"

Carefully, the three girls squeezed through the pen gate so as not to let any baby zebras escape.

Briana chose the smallest zebra baby. He walked right up to her, eying the baby bottle hungrily. She held the bottle above his head and tilted it. "Is this right?" she called.

"That's perfect," Akua called back.

The baby zebra was already sucking at the bottle nipple. He was surprisingly strong for a baby. Briana had to hold the bottle tightly to keep him from yanking it away. Briana was thrilled! She was actually feeding a baby zebra! It was an incredible feeling to know that she was caring for a baby animal that needed her help.

Marissa was having the same experience. An older, bigger baby was sucking at her bottle. Marissa had to use both hands to keep her from pulling it away. "This is so cool!" Marissa called. "I can't wait to tell all my GlobalFriends what it's like to feed a real baby zebra! I've never experienced anything like this!"

It took hardly any time at all to feed all ten baby zebras. As Briana's last zebra drained the bottle dry, she looked over to where Akua was feeding her last baby zebra and frowned. Akua was listening intently to two men. They were standing outside the zebra pen, talking excitedly. They looked like tourists,

American tourists, in expensive safari clothes. Briana had just started over when they walked off quickly toward the Animal Orphanage exit.

"What's going on?" Briana called.

Akua looked over. Briana could see that her quiet friend was very excited. "Come, I will tell you!"

Briana and Marissa joined Akua at the zebra pen gate, squeezing back through carefully.

"One of those men spotted two baby giraffes on the far side of the park near the Athi Basin. There are no other giraffes around for kilometers. He thinks they have been abandoned," Akua explained as they gathered up the empty bottles.

"What's a kilometer?" Marissa whispered to Briana.

"Like a mile, I think, but shorter," Briana whispered back.

"I will talk to Makos. He is my uncle. Maybe he can arrange for us to go along on the rescue." Akua was already striding toward the main hut. Briana and Marissa had to race after her. "We must hurry," she yelled, breaking into a run.

"Why?" Marissa called.

"Because orphaned babies can wander off or even be killed by another animal," Akua shouted.

Briana and Marissa stared. "Oh, my gosh! Let's go!"

They were out of breath by the time they reached the main hut. Akua ran to a tall, slim young man. "Uncle Makos, let me tell you what I just heard!"

Makos looked down with a friendly smile. "What is that?"

Akua related her story quickly, but Makos was ahead of her. She had barely finished describing the two men when he called five other park rangers together to form a rescue party.

"Uncle Makos, can we help in any way?" Akua pleaded.

Makos grinned. "And who are 'we'?"

"My GlobalFriends" Akua pointed. "I told you they were coming to Kenya. And me, of course. We won't get in the way."

Makos patted her cheek, but he wasn't smiling any more. "I know you're very good to have along on rescues especially with giraffes, but do your friends know what to do?"

"No, but they could learn. Today they could just watch. Please, Uncle Makos? This is the first time they've ever been to Kenya. Please?" Akua pleaded.

Makos was thinking as the rescue team headed out the door. He made up his mind very suddenly. "All right. But you must all be very quiet and stay in the jeep. You too, Akua. Stay with your friends."

"Yessssss!" Marissa exclaimed. She and Briana jumped up in the air and clapped their hands together in a triumphant high five. "Yesssssss!"

"The adventure begins," Briana whispered eagerly. She could hardly wait!

Rescue

"There they are," Makos said quietly into the walky-talky radio in his hand. Standing in the open air jeep, he pointed off to the left. The driver of the other jeep grinned and turned the wheel sharply, veering off to the left. The jeep with Makos and the three GlobalFriends followed a bit more cautiously. Makos was still standing, bouncing as they traveled over the rough terrain. He was hanging onto the top of the windshield. The girls were in the backseat, anxious for the baby giraffes. The truck towing the animal trailer was way behind.

Searching, Briana could see two tiny giraffe heads on long necks above the grassland scrub. Marissa nudged her. "Is that them?" she whispered, pointing in the other direction. They were adorable, but they looked frightened.

Briana looked where Marissa was pointing. Two, no, three more heads appeared above the grassy scrub by some bottle-shaped trees. Whatever they were, they seemed to be leaping up in the air! She

stared. They sure didn't look like giraffes. They weren't giraffes!

Briana tugged at Akua's sleeve. "What's that?" She was scared and her voice sounded urgent.

Akua quickly turned, and her face tightened. She leaned forward and grabbed the back of Makos' shirt. "Look!"

Makos stared, his face grim. *"Fisi.* Hyenas." He started talking into the walky-talky radio again. "We have hyenas to the right, just behind those baobab trees. Circle to the left. We'll go right."

The driver of their jeep had been listening. He slowed and turned off to the right, circling back toward the baobab trees.

"What's wrong?" Marissa whispered.

Akua looked tense. She spoke quietly. "Hyenas will kill the baby giraffes for food."

Marissa and Briana looked to each other. Oh no! They sat back on the jeep seat, anxious and worried.

Their jeep was approaching the baobab trees. Suddenly four hyenas leaped up and took off running. Briana and Marissa had never seen hyenas out in the wild before. They looked really strange with their sloping backs and short hind legs, especially when they were running and leaping through the brush. The hyenas were fast!

Both jeeps chased after them, bouncing and jouncing over the rough savannah. Marissa, Briana and Akua hung onto the passenger straps in the backseat for dear life!

At one point, it seemed like the pack of hyenas might split up and go back for the baby giraffes. The driver of their jeep slammed on the brakes, and Marissa held her breath. Then the lead hyena gave a short, harsh bark, and all four hyenas dashed on ahead again.

Jamming his foot down on the accelerator, the driver of their jeep raced after them. Still hanging onto the windshield with one hand, Makos stretched over and leaned on the jeep horn. The sharp, continuous blare split the air. Makos leaned on the horn again. With a burst of panicked speed, all four hyenas sprinted out of sight.

Briana let out a huge sigh. She'd been holding her breath too. "Now the baby giraffes are okay, aren't they?"

Akua looked a little relieved, but not completely. "Those hyenas won't get them, but there are other dangers. We need to get them to safety."

The jeeps circled around to

where they had seen the baby giraffes. The three friends watched from the backseat as the park rangers climbed down and spread out. They moved very slowly and carefully.

Circling the baby giraffes, the men rustled tin pans filled with grain at the babies. Curious and hungry, the two babies crept forward. Their ears were pricked straight up, listening. Hesitantly, they stretched their long necks out, nibbling at the grain.

Cautiously, Makos and another park ranger slid lead ropes around their necks. Both babies yanked back, terrified, kicking in the air. Makos was talking gently, patting the babies, soothing them. He was very gentle with the giraffes. Finally, the babies were calm enough to slip halters over their heads and lead them into the animal trailer.

"Whew!" Briana exclaimed, clapping a sweaty hand to her forehead. "I've never been so scared!"

Akua was smiling. "You get used to it. I did."

"Is it always like this?" Marissa had been scared too. She loved animals and hated to see them scared or hurt.

"Almost always, yes. There are many animals in Kenya who prey on weak, orphaned babies. It's nature's way. It is why we have an Animal Orphanage now. We try to protect as many as we can." Akua was looking serious again. She glanced around, trying to locate Makos.

He was standing off a little ways, pulling apart a thin, weedy-looking thicket of thorn bushes. He gestured to one of the men in the rescue party to come and look.

Makos and the other man made their way back to the two jeeps slowly, talking all the while.

Everybody gathered around the jeeps. His face grim, Makos was talking about the animal trap he had found.

"Poachers," Akua whispered to Briana and Marissa.

"What's a 'poacher'?" Briana whispered back.

"Anyone who hunts animals illegally. In Kenya, it's illegal to hunt animals anywhere. My Uncle Makos found an animal trap that was set by poachers. Poaching is common in the Nairobi National Park because we have so many animals. Hunters want the animals' fur or tusks to sell," Akua explained.

"What is Makos gonna do?" Briana whispered.

"Usually we leave the trap as it is, but watch to see who comes to check it," Akua whispered.

"So you can catch 'em redhanded!" Marissa guessed.

Akua nodded. "Exactly."

Makos was grinning broadly again. "I found the trap, so I'll take the first watch."

"You should go back to make sure the new giraffes are settled," one of the rescue team members protested. "I can take the first watch."

"The baby giraffes will be fine," Makos asserted, "especially with Akua there to make sure." He knew Akua was completely trustworthy.

Akua smiled. *"Ahsanta sana,* Uncle Makos. Thanks. You can depend on me."

Briana looked back as their jeep pulled away. Standing in the grassy scrub with two water canteens slung around his neck, Makos smiled and waved.

The girls waved back. Akua tried to look brave but Marissa and Briana both noticed a worried look on her face.

Hungry Baby Giraffes

"We should prepare four bottles," Akua instructed, pulling a different bottle of white powder off the feeding station shelf. "This is the mother's milk substitute for giraffes." She handed the big bottle to Marissa. "Mix it half powder and half water."

"Is it different than the milk substitute for zebras?" Marissa was measuring the powder.

"A little, yes. All the babies have different formulas." Akua handed four clean baby bottles to Briana.

Briana unscrewed the bottle tops. "How can you tell them all apart?" She was eager to know.

"You have to be very careful to read the label." Akua poured some of the milk into a bottle.

"Do you think they're going to catch the animal poachers?" Briana handed the bottle top to Akua.

"Sometimes we do." Akua screwed on the nipple top.

"What happens then?" Marissa was curious.

"They are sent to prison. Unfortunately, often poachers are here from other countries. If they get out of Kenya without being caught, it is very difficult to catch them." Akua filled the last of the four bottles and fit the cap on snugly. "Come, let's go feed the new babies."

In the new baby giraffe pen, Akua dragged in two bales of straw. She positioned them about six feet apart and climbed up on one of them. "Like this, you have to get high enough to make them reach up for it."

Standing on top of the straw bale, Akua held out her bottle of milk and made chirping noises to get their attention. Both baby giraffes pricked up their ears.

"You go first," Briana whispered to Marissa. "I'll feed the second bottle of milk to her."

Marissa scrambled up on the straw bale.

One of the baby giraffes had already come over to Akua. He sniffed at the milk bottle, then hungrily fastened his mouth on the nipple.

Briana could hear slurping sounds as the second baby cautiously

walked up. Marissa held the bottle exactly as she'd seen Akua do. The second baby was sniffing at the bottle too. He started sucking. Hard! Marissa giggled. Frantic eyes wide, the startled baby giraffe yanked back.

"It's okay," Marissa murmured soothingly. "It's all right."

The baby giraffe tiptoed forward on four thin, spindly legs.

Marissa held out the bottle. "It's okay." The baby giraffe fastened his mouth on the nipple again, and she sighed in relief.

The giraffes finished both of their bottles and were looking for thirds when Akua signalled Briana and Marissa. "Keep them in the far corner while I drag out the straw."

"They look like they're still hungry," Marissa observed.

"We don't want to overfeed them," Akua explained as she wedged the gate open. "Two bottles is plenty." She dragged the straw bales out.

Marissa and Briana joined her outside the pen.

"There's one thing I still don't get," Marissa said, puzzled. "How come poachers poach?"

Akua led the way back to the feeding station hut with the empty bottles. "Many of our animals are very valuable. Sometimes they trap them alive and sell them to zoos because some zoos don't care where they get their animals. They don't care if it's against the law."

Marissa swallowed hard. "That's awful."

Akua nodded. "But it's not as bad as killing."

"They kill them too?" Briana was shocked.

"Poachers will kill a *tembo*," Akua said slowly, explaining, "a *tembo* is an elephant."

"Why?" Marissa was aghast.

"For their valuable ivory tusks, even though selling ivory is illegal. Ivory can be used for many things. Expensive jewelry and carvings." Akua frowned. "Poachers can be very dangerous. I worry for Uncle Makos out there alone. I've been thinking. What if those men I heard talking here before were  the poachers? What if they're poaching baby animals? What if they're stealing our babies?"

At times like this, Briana counted on her steadfast faith. "Makos knows what he's doing. He'll be fine. And if those poachers are stealing baby animals, we'll catch them. And put them in jail forever!"

Akua hoped she was right.

Market Day At Nakuru

"You're still worried about your uncle, aren't you?" Briana asked. The next day the girls and their mothers were exploring the huge outdoor market at Nakuru.

Akua turned from the display of African drums. "A little."

Marissa looped an arm through hers. "Don't worry. He'll be okay. Look Akua, these are great baskets!"

Briana, Marissa, Akua and their moms were having great fun. The Nakuru market was huge, and it seemed like everything was for sale! Food and masks, drums and jewelry, clothing and blankets, even furniture! There were games and toys. And everything was all spread out. And it was noisy and busy, and there were dozens of little gray monkeys with black faces chattering and squealing in the trees!

"I know what we can do," Briana suggested. "Let's put together a package of foods that Makos likes. Then we can take it back to the Animal Orphanage so it'll be there when he returns. He'll be hungry by then, and he'll have all his favorite stuff waiting for him!"

Akua loved the idea! "Let's get some blankets too! In case he has to go back out in the bush."

"Cool! What does he like?" Marissa was excited again, glad to have a purpose.

"I know he likes *mandazi, tende* and *maemba.* Oh, sorry, I forgot that you don't speak *Kiswahili. Mandazi* are like your doughnuts. *Tende* and *maemba* are dates and mangoes. We should get some *nyama choma* too, that's barbecued goat's meat and *ugali...*"

Briana broke in, "I've heard of *ugali.* What is it?"

"A thick corn meal mush," Akua explained. "We eat it almost every day."

"Goat's meat?" Marissa was skeptical. "And corn meal mush? That's different!"

"Oh, I know! We'll get a pineapple, *mananasi.* Makos loves *mananasi!*" Akua added to their list.

"Where do we get all this stuff?" Briana was eager to start.

"Follow me!" Akua grabbed their hands and took off at a lope through the crowded market.

At the blanket stall, Briana had a great idea. "Hey, Akua! You know how we're gonna celebrate Kwanzaa? How 'bout if we ask your Uncle Makos if he wants to join us? I bet he'd really like it!"

Akua was examining a blanket. She turned around. Her eyes were shining. "I was hoping you would want to invite him!"

"This'll be cool!" Marissa joined in. "I bet Makos knows a bunch of really awesome stuff about Africa. Not that you don't," she hastened to tell Akua, "but he knows about it from a guy's point of view."

Akua's eyes were twinkling. She knew that her Uncle Makos had many stories to tell.

Briana grabbed a blanket. "Let's get this stuff back to the Animal Orphanage! We can tell him all about Kwanzaa and make sure he can come!"

Makos Disappears

Back at the Animal Orphanage, Briana carried a basket with all the food while Akua and Marissa carried the blankets.

"We'll go to the main hut," Akua decided. "If Uncle Makos is back, he'll probably be there."

The girls entered the main hut. A woman sat at a table near the door, and a group of men stood talking at the far end.

"*Jambo.* Is Makos here?" Akua asked. "Is he back?"

An odd look crossed the woman's face. "*Hapana.*"

"No? When will he be back?" Akua pressed.

The woman shook her head, a peculiar look on her face. Akua whirled around, spilling the blanket. "Something's wrong!"

She raced across the large hut and tugged at the nearest park ranger's arm. "Where is Makos?"

Surprised, the man turned. "How do you know of Makos?"

"My uncle stayed in the bush to watch the poacher's trap!"

The man nodded. "That is true. Unfortunately, when Nachi

here went to take his place this morning, he could not find Makos or the poacher's trap."

"What?!" Akua was stunned. "Makos is gone! Where?"

"We are going to search for him. These men will find him," the man promised. He turned, speaking *Kiswahili* to the men.

Akua tugged again. "Please, I must go with you!"

The man turned, his stern face softening. "Little one, a search party is no place for a child. Poachers are dangerous."

"I know! That's why I want to help!" Akua insisted.

"No, little one." The man turned back to his search party.

Akua yanked at his shirt determinedly. "You need me!"

He turned again, sighing. "What are you saying, little one?"

"You need me! Makos and I have secret symbols we use to tell each other where we are!" Akua was close to tears.

"What?" The man was listening now.

"Symbols. We use them in the Animal Orphanage to tell each other which animals have been fed and watered and where we're going next. It saves time." Akua was desperate to help. "He may have left a message. A message only I can read!"

The man frowned. "You could draw the symbols and tell me what they mean. If Makos left a message, I could read it."

"It would take time! The men who saw the baby giraffes might be the poachers. I could identify them!" Akua cried.

The man quickly made up his mind. "You can go as far as the original poacher's trap site. No further! If we find any messages there, you can help us. Then you must return here. The bush is no place for children when poachers are around."

Akua agreed. It was better than not being able to help at all! "My friends must come too," she insisted quietly. The man started to protest, but Akua was adamant. "We need all the help we can get searching for messages Makos may have left. They can help to look for his symbols. I need them!"

Despite the danger, the park ranger agreed. By now, the poachers could be far from the original trap site. They could be anywhere! With apprehension and determination, the search party set off.

The Search Begins

It seemed to take forever to reach the trap site. In fact, Briana wasn't sure it was the trap site. The sprawling savannah looked all the same!

It wasn't until they pulled up and stopped in the same spot as they parked the day before that she realized they were there. "This is so confusing," she whispered. "How can they tell where we are?"

Still tense, Akua smiled anyway. "If you lived here your whole life you would find it easy. You see that ridge?" She pointed to the outcropping of rocks in front of them. "And that stand of baobab trees? And that hill? We're almost in the center of it all. That thorn thicket is where my Uncle Makos found the trap." She gestured to the scrubby thicket to the left of the jeep and started to climb out. The park rangers in the search party had already scattered, looking for tracks or signs of a struggle. Or anything at all!

From twenty feet away, the search party leader shouted something to Akua in *Kiswahili*. Akua nodded.

"What'd he say?" Marissa whispered.

"A warning to be careful." Akua glanced around. "All of us. Come, help me look for a message. It could be scratched on a rock or dug in a tree trunk. He may have drawn it in the dirt."

"What are we looking for?" Briana quizzed as she and Marissa clambered out of the jeep. "What kind of symbols?"

"The symbol for Makos is a lion's head. Like this." Akua quickly sketched a rough lion's head with a wild mane in the Kenyan dirt. "My symbol is a giraffe. Like this." She drew a long-necked, four-legged creature in the dirt beside the lion head. "Spread out." She was already stepping away. "But not too far. Be careful of snakes. Keep a lookout for wild animals."

Twenty minutes later, Marissa gave a shout. "Look what I found!" She was swinging one of the canteens over her head.

Akua and Briana came running.

"Why would he leave a water canteen?" Briana yelled, scrambling through the scrub. "Doesn't he need the water?"

"An empty canteen is of no use," Akua huffed as they ran up. She was desperately hoping that it was empty.

Marissa's face fell. "It's not empty." She shook the water canteen. They could hear water sloshing. "It's full."

Akua's eyes closed as her shoulders sank in despair.

Briana took her hand and squeezed it. "Have faith," she whispered. Faith always comforted Briana.

Akua's voice was low. "The poachers have captured Makos, I know it. They have killed my uncle by now."

"I don't think so," Briana disagreed. "I think he's following them. That's why he's not here. He's tracking them."

Akua brightened. "Maybe he has gone after them."

"I'm sure of it!" Marissa exclaimed, always optimistic. "Come on, let's look again. I bet we missed his message!"

The three girls scattered. This time Briana went left, Marissa went right and Akua went behind the jeep.

Suddenly Akua cried out, "Here! Here it is!"

From all over, heads popped up. Briana and Marissa reached Akua's side first. The rangers weren't far behind.

Akua was bending over a rock, trying to read the message scratched on the top. "Marissa, could you stand over there? That puts a shadow on the rock. I can see the symbols better."

Marissa quickly moved. "Is here okay?"

Akua nodded, concentrating. She traced the symbols scratched on the rock with her hand. "You see this? This is my symbol. The giraffe. And this is a trap. That means the poachers. This jeep must mean the poachers have a jeep. And these two are trucks with animal trailers. The poachers must be capturing live animals, otherwise they would not need trailers."

Akua was puzzling over the last two symbols.

One looked like a sun, but it could have been a moon. Briana couldn't tell if it was setting or rising. Akua was wondering the same thing. Marissa thought it might be a ball. Or a face. Or a pie. Or even a doorknob!

The very last symbol looked like a bucket. Briana frowned. What could that mean? Maybe Makos meant water. Like a lake. Were the poachers heading toward a lake? Which one? Maybe it was a feed bucket. Maybe something to do with food. Maybe a market, like at Nakuru. Or maybe it was a pail. For digging. Or carrying stuff. Dirt or sand maybe. Marissa sighed. This was going to be hard. Really hard.

"Let me see." Akua exclaimed. "This," she pointed to the bucket, "is a water bucket. At the Orphanage, the last thing we do at night is fill the water buckets. So this," she touched the sun, "must be an evening sun. A setting sun. And the sun sets in the west. The poachers and Makos have gone west!"

The search party leader looked at Akua admiringly. "Good work!" He said something in *Kiswahili* to the search party members, and they all headed toward the jeeps. The leader turned to Akua. "Chagos in the first jeep will take you and your friends back to the Orphanage."

"Not yet!" Akua protested. "You may need me again!"

The search party leader frowned. "You agreed to go back."

"Not until I know that Uncle Makos is safe," Akua insisted.

"That was not our understanding."

"Please? I know I can be of help. There may be more messages. Only I will understand them. Please?" Akua begged.

The search party leader frowned, but relented. "All right. You and your friends may come further. But be warned. You must do as I say, and the next time I tell you to return, you must go. No discussion!"

Happy to agree, Akua smiled. "Next time, no discussion. We will do as you say."

With renewed determination, they climbed back into the jeeps. Hugging the water canteen tightly, Akua scanned the horizon for any sign of her uncle.

Hunting The Poachers

It was almost an hour later. The two jeeps in the search party came to a slow halt. Up ahead was a hill with more baobab trees off to the left side. Briana gazed around. The savannah's of Kenya stretched for miles with only occasional hills and groves of bottle-shaped baobab trees.

"What are we stopping for?" Marissa whispered.

Akua shook her head, puzzled.

The leader of the search party turned around from the front seat. "Be very quiet," he cautioned. "The poachers may be behind the hill ahead. It's the first hill we've come to that's high enough to hide behind. We are going to climb it on foot... Not you!" he whispered sternly as Akua started to climb out of the jeep. "You three girls stay here with Nachi!" He nodded toward the driver of their jeep. "Out of danger! If the poachers are there, we want to take them by surprise!"

Akua sat down. "Yes, sir," she said quietly.

The search party leader climbed out and started up the hill. All six men from the other jeep joined him.

The seven men silently climbed the hill. Toward the top, they all crouched. At the very top, they were lying in the grass, peering over the hilltop. They stayed there for a long time.

"What are they looking at?" Briana was getting impatient.

"Maybe the poachers are on the other side of the hill," Akua guessed.

"Why don't they go get 'em?" Marissa demanded.

Akua voiced her scariest thought. "Perhaps they are holding Makos hostage."

The girls stared at her. "I didn't think about that!" Marissa admitted. "What would they do to him? Never mind," she said hastily. "I don't really want to know."

Briana was listening to the sounds of the Kenyan countryside. There was something that didn't sound quite right. Some kind of bird call, she thought. What was it? Briana frowned. It wasn't right. She nudged Akua. "What's that sound?" The bird call echoed again. "That one! What's that?"

Akua glanced toward the baobab trees. "A flamingo. It's just a flamingo."

Marissa whipped around. "Out here? There's no water out here! We're miles from any lakes!"

A look of surprise crossed Akua's face. "You're right" she said slowly. "We're many kilometers from any lake." Suddenly, Akua

47

stood. "Maybe it's Makos!"

They were gazing all around when suddenly Akua pointed to the grove of baobab trees. "There! Makos is there! In that tree! See him! Just over halfway up!"

Briana opened her mouth to call to Makos, but Nachi stopped her. "Sssshhhhhh! The poachers!"

Briana swallowed her greeting, looking sheepish. "Sorry."

"What now?" Marissa asked eagerly, ready for action.

"He may be hurt," Nachi whispered quietly. "I will go to him." He climbed out of the jeep.

"We're going with you," Akua decided. "Come on."

Crouching, the park ranger and three girls made their way through the grass to the trees.

By the time they got to the trees, Makos had climbed down. "Akua! What are you doing here?" he whispered. Akua hugged him so hard, he nearly fell down. Sinking to his knees in the tall grass, Makos grinned at Marissa and Briana.

Tears were shining in Akua's eyes. "We thought the poachers were going to hurt you."

Makos laughed quietly. "Not me!"

"But you didn't come back." Marissa was close to tears too.

Makos nodded. "I was tracking them." He pointed over the hill. "They are there with their animal traps and trailers." Makos glanced at Briana and Marissa.

"I hope you catch them," Briana said quietly with conviction.

They could hear rustling in the grass coming toward them. Akua turned a frightened face to Makos. "What's that?"

Silently, Makos and Nachi scooted all three girls behind the baobab trees. Peering around a smooth tree trunk, Briana could see the other park rangers as they emerged from the tall grasses. The three girls crept out as the men greeted Nachi and Makos.

"We should take photographs of the poacher's vehicles," Makos was saying, "for identification later. Where is the camera?"

The lead park ranger shook his head. In their haste to begin the search for Makos, the rangers had forgotten a camera.

"I've got a camera," Briana volunteered quietly. She took her camera everywhere so she wouldn't ever forget anything. "It's in the jeep."

The group of rangers and girls made their way back to the jeeps. The leader was talking to Makos. "I want you to use one of the jeeps and take the girls back to the Animal Orphanage now. We cannot endanger them further."

Makos started to protest, but the ranger held up his hand. "You've done enough. You tracked the poachers and led us here. We can take over now."

Makos nodded slowly as Briana handed her camera to the park ranger. "Come girls. He is right. We can do no more here."

Celebrating Kwanzaa

The next day, Briana leaned forward and tugged at Makos' sleeve. "We're all waiting! What happened to the poachers?"

Makos laughed and turned around from the front seat of the *matatu*. "I was going to wait until we get to Akua's house to tell you. Then I won't have to tell the story twice."

Briana sank back, disappointed. "Oh."

"Rats!" Marissa was anxious to hear too.

Briana's and Marissa's mothers were interested to hear the outcome also.

Mako's eyes were twinkling. "I will tell you this much..." He paused dramatically. "We caught them!"

"Good!" Briana exclaimed, gratified that justice was served.

Marissa was laughing with delight. "Super awesome!"

The *matatu* pulled up and stopped as Akua stepped out the door of the nearest house. *"Jambo! Karibu!* Welcome!"

Marissa and Briana grabbed the bags of Kwanzaa preparations

and scrambled out. Their mothers and Makos followed a bit more slowly carrying baskets piled high with food.

Marissa raced up to Akua. "This is where you live? It's so cool!" She was staring in wide-eyed amazement. All around the small village were round mud houses with grass-thatched roofs. Akua's home had geometric shapes painted all around the outside wall. Some were red, some orange, some green.

"Very cool," Briana added.

Akua took one of the Kwanzaa decoration bags and led the way into the simple mud house. "We used to live in Nairobi," she explained, hefting the heavy bag up onto the decorated tabletop. "But we moved back here to the countryside two years ago. My mother and father were both born in this village. Being a part of the tribe is very important to all Africans." She nodded to Briana. "Of course, you know that."

Briana nodded firmly. "Absolutely."

Makos and the girls mothers paused in the doorway.

Akua's mother hurried forward to greet him. "Jambo. Welcome to our home. Please, come in. I have prepared tea. Make yourselves comfortable." She gestured around the inside of the house. Simple wooden furniture was decorated with geometric designs in brilliant colors. The base of the table was an extraordinary carved elephant!

All three girls perched on stools around Makos with cups of Kenyan tea. "Now you can tell us," Briana announced. "Everybody's here. What happened?"

Makos sat on a stool too. "Weelllll...", he drawled.

"Hurry!" Marissa commanded, tugging on his pantleg.

Makos laughed again. "Let's see. After we left, the rangers crept up the hill again in the jeep..."

"To surprise them!" Briana told her mother.

Makos nodded. "Yes, to surprise the poachers. And they did surprise them. It was easy to catch the poachers driving the trucks with the animal trailers because they were too heavy to go very fast across the savannah..."

"What happened to the animals in the trailers?" Marissa encouraged.

Makos looked somber. "They're all in the Animal Orphanage."

"We can take good care of them!" Akua cried.

He nodded. "Yes Akua, we'll need to. It was all baby animals inside their trailers. Zebras, gazelles and giraffes."

Marissa spoke up. "We can help you with the baby animals.

When can we start?"

Makos finished his tea. He glanced at Marissa and bounced to his feet. "Tomorrow is soon enough. I thought this was a celebration! Let's have some fun! What's in the bags?"

Briana got to her feet. "The Kwanzaa preparations."

"Kwanzaa?" Makos peeked inside one of the bags.

Briana grinned. "For our Kwanzaa celebration. You'll see! You get to help."

Full of questions, the girls and Makos unpacked the bags.

"What's this?" Makos drew out the Kwanzaa flag. It had broad green, red and black stripes.

Briana held it open. "It's to fly outside, to show everyone we're celebrating Kwanzaa. It's Kwanzaa colors. See, the black symbolizes African people, the green symbolizes our hope and the African land, and the red symbolizes our struggle."

"Cool," Marissa whispered.

"I'll hang it." Stroking the flag, Makos stepped outside.

"What's this?" Marissa held up the straw mat.

"Oh, put that in the center of the table. The handwoven mat stands for our past." Briana helped her lay it flat.

"Three ears of corn?" Akua was holding them up.

Briana grinned as Makos walked back into the mud house. "To symbolize the children. That's us. Lay them on the mat."

Marissa drew out the candle holder.

"That's a Kinara. It symbolizes all African Americans, both past and present. I brought candles too." Briana fit the seven candles into the candle-holder and placed it on the straw mat. "The seven candles stand for the seven principles of Kwanzaa."

"We did pretty good living by the principles of Kwanzaa this week, didn't we?" Marissa was adding the Unity cup to the other items on the straw mat.

"Yes, we did." Briana said softly, "especially pulling together. We were great at the Animal Orphanage."

"And when we were searching for Makos and the poachers. That was cool," Marissa put in.

Akua nodded firmly. "Even at the Nakuru market when we were all pulling together to gather food for Uncle Makos."

"Briana's been trying very hard to follow all the Kwanzaa principles," her mother commented. "Thinking for herself is one of the things Briana does best. If it hadn't been for Briana, we might never have come back to Kenya. Briana always stands up for what she believes in, and she believes in our heritage."

Briana laughed. "Even if I do make you crazy sometimes." She looked at all the happy faces. "I think the easiest principle to follow is having faith. I've had faith for a long time that we would come to Kenya."

"And you always had faith that my Uncle Makos would be safe," Akua added. "I have faith that we'll be friends forever."

Marissa linked arms with her two best friends. "And I have faith that everyone will be *rafikis*. Friends forever. All over the world. GlobalFriends everywhere!"

NAIROBI NATIONAL PARK ANIMAL ORPHANAGE

To preserve precious wildlife, Kenya has developed a magnificent system of parks where you can watch from the safety of your vehicle while the wild animals roam free. Elephants and cheetahs are two of the animals you might see on safari in Kenya.

Safari. Kenya is a popular tourist spot. Visitors travel the huge animal reserves, enjoying the wild animals all around. The only shooting is done with a camera. Killing or trapping wild animals is illegal in Kenya.

Animal Orphanage. Just inside the Nairobi National Park is an Animal Orphanage. Lost or abandoned baby animals are nursed to health as they grow to adulthood, when they are healthy and old enough, the animals are released back into the wild.

African Animals. East Africa is the home of the largest number of big mammals in the world. In Kenya, you'll see lions, cheetahs, monkeys, zebras, giraffes, elephants, rhinoceros, flamingoes, vultures, hyenas, gazelles and lots more.

Savannah. Most of Kenya is grassland, called savannah. That's why there are so many wild animals. But Kenya also has desert, snowy mountains, and city streets.

Kanga. Kangas are long, rectangular pieces of cloth that are wrapped around the body. These wraps are beautiful with their bright colors and bold patterns. *Masai* girls especially like red.

Masai. The *Masai* are an ethnic group in Kenya. Most *Masai* live in small villages and make their living by farming.

Thatched Hut. In Kenya's countryside, there are traditional houses made of local materials. The most common structure is the round mud house with a dried-grass thatched roof which keeps it cool in Kenya's warm climate.

THE MARKET AT LAKE NAKURU

Market Day at Lake Nakuru is crowded and festive. You can find everything like masks, drums, food, and jewelry right out in the open air with monkeys chattering in the trees above. Be sure to make a side trip to Lake Nakuru to see the flamingoes.

Markets. Many Kenyans are farmers. They grow food for their families to eat and sell the rest of their crops at markets. Traders also come to the market providing a range of products including clothing, baskets, fabrics and more displayed right out in the open air.

Gele. A kerchief or *gele* is a cloth head covering. It is a long scarf that is wrapped around the head. A *gele* may be worn by African women to market and as part of a festive dress.

Masks. During traditional dances, Africans wear highly stylized masks and headdresses. Tourists like to buy these kinds of masks at the market.

Drums. The drum is a very important musical instrument in Africa. There are many different types of drums made from many different types of materials including tree trunks and clay.

Mankala. *Mankala* is a counting board game Kenyans play. It's a variation of the game Checkers. The names and rules vary from region to region.

Lake Nakuru Flamingos. The eighteen-square-mile, heart-shaped Lake Nakuru attracts more flamingos that any other body of water on earth. At times, you can see more than two million flamingos gathered there.

Monkeys. Some Kenyan monkeys are very shy, but not the playful Vervet. Extremely inquisitive, Vervets are usually found in groups of up to 30. If you're out on safari, Vervets will come right inside your tent in search of a handout!

Clay Pottery. For many years, Africans have used clay to make tools, pottery, ornaments, jewelry, and utensils. Today, many Africans still make clay pottery by hand, using traditional methods and designs.

Global Friends
ADVENTURES

The new GlobalFriends adventure books have it ALL : excitement, thrills, ghosts, exotic sights, sounds... anything is possible when GlobalFriends kids travel around the world solving mystery after mystery. GlobalFriends kids show their smarts talking on the internet, writing letters, and using teamwork to crack each case. And that's just the beginning! When the GlobalFriends travel to countries they've barely heard of before, they are amazed at what they uncover! Rain forest treasures, ancient Egyptian codes, haunted German castles! And, they discover how kids live in different countries; what they eat, what they like to do, how they think!

"I'd like to say that I found the text outstanding. These books give kids the opportunity to appreciate other cultures while enjoying reading at the same time."
— Third Grade Teacher, New Jersey

How many GlobalFriends Adventures have you read?

- ☐ The Secret Egyptian Code
- ☐ The Haunted English Riding Stable
- ☐ The Mystery of the Russian Circus School
- ☐ The Missing Japanese Festival Dolls
- ☐ Discovery in a French Garden
- ☐ Rescue in Kenya
- ☐ The Ghostly German Castle
- ☐ The Chinese New Year Dragon
- ☐ The Lost Treasure of the Rain Forest

To order, call 1-800-393-5421

Global ❤ Friends™

Discover the world of GlobalFriends multi-cultural, educational play program. Children 6-12 are spellbound by colorful GlobalFriends international dolls, hand-crafted accessories, panoramic playkits, adventure books, videos, and the GlobalFriends Club.

International Doll Collection: GlobalFriends dolls have their own unique stories to share about their country. The 14" soft vinyl dolls are fully articulated and have colorful traditional and modern costumes. Their imaginative accessories, including bazaar tents, river boats and snow sleighs create a fascinating learning experience. They even have fuzzy pets!

Scenic Panoramic PlayKits: The playkits set the scene with colorfully painted backdrops of the country's landmarks, celebrations and people. Adding to the experience is an activit book of fantasy play crafts, fun facts and vocabulary.

GlobalFriends Videos: Entertaining, educational videos explore a day in the life of a real 10 year old living in another country. Learn what kids eat, what their school is like, what they like to do. Discover the country and culture from the inside out.

GlobalFriends Club: Learning about the world becomes REAL through the GlobalFriends Club. Kids connect with other kids around the world through Club newsletters, international pen pals and the GlobalFriends web site, **http://www.globalfriends.com.**

FREE CATALOG
1-800-393-5421

Kenyan Vocabulary Words

Kenyan	English
Jambo	Hello
Karibu	Welcome
Matatu	Minibus taxi
Rafiki	Friend
Kanga	Traditional clothing
Gele	Headwrap
Swahili /Kiswahili	Official language
Twiga	Giraffe
Kifaru	Rhinoceros
Punda milia	Zebra
Ahsante sana	Thank you
Hapana	No
Ndiyo	Yes